PUFFIN BOOKS

Dinosaur
School

Dinosaur School

Dick King-Smith

Illustrated by
Tim Warnes

PUFFIN BOOKS

For Charlotte - T. W.

PUFFIN BOOKS

Published by the Penguin Group
Penguin Books Ltd, 27 Wrights Lane, London W8 5TZ, England
Penguin Putnam Inc., 375 Hudson Street, New York, New York 10014, USA
Penguin Books Australia Ltd, Ringwood, Victoria, Australia
Penguin Books Canada Ltd, 10 Alcorn Avenue, Toronto, Ontario, Canada M4V 3B2
Penguin Books (NZ) Ltd, Private Bag 102902, NSMC, Auckland, New Zealand

On the World Wide Web at: www.penguin.com

Penguin Books Ltd, Registered Offices: Harmondsworth, Middlesex, England

This title was originally published as 'Use Your Brains'
in *A Narrow Squeak and Other Animal Stories* by Viking 1993
This edition published in Puffin Books 1999
3 5 7 9 10 8 6 4 2

Text copyright © Fox Busters, 1993
Illustrations copyright © Tim Warnes, 1999
All rights reserved

The moral right of the author and illustrator has been asserted

Set in Bembo Schoolbook

Printed in Hong Kong by Midas Printing Ltd

British Library Cataloguing in Publication Data
A CIP catalogue record for this book is available from
the British Library

ISBN 0–141–30187–2

Little Basil Brontosaurus came home
from his first morning at playschool in
floods of tears.

"Whatever's the matter, darling?"
said his mother, whose name was
Araminta. "Why are you crying?"

"They've been teasing me," sobbed
Basil.

"Who have? The other children?"

A variety of little dinosaurs went to the playschool. There were diplodocuses, iguanodons, ankylosauruses and many others. Basil was the only young brontosaurus.

"Yes," sniffed Basil. "They said I was stupid. They said I hadn't got a brain in my head."

At this point Basil's father, a forty-tonne brontosaurus who measured twenty-seven metres from nose to tail-tip, came lumbering up through the shallows of the lake in which the family lived.

"Herb!" called Araminta. "Did you hear that? The kids at playschool said our Basil hadn't a brain in his head."

Herb considered this while pulling up and swallowing large amounts of waterweed.

"He has," he said at last. "Hasn't he?"

"Of course you have, darling," said Araminta to her little son. "Come along with me now, and dry your tears and listen carefully."

Still snivelling, Basil waded into the lake. He followed his mother to a quiet spot, well away from the other dinosaurs that were feeding around the shallows.

Araminta settled herself where the water was deep enough to help support her enormous bulk.

"Now listen to Mummy, Basil darling," she said. "What I'm about to tell you is a secret.

Every brontosaurus that ever hatched is told this secret by his or her mummy or daddy, once he or she is old enough. One day you'll be grown up, and you'll have a wife of your own, and she'll lay eggs, and then you'll have babies. And when those babies are old enough, they'll have to be told, just like I'm going to tell you."

"Tell me what?" said Basil.

"Promise not to breathe a word of it to the other children?"

"All right. But what is it?"

"It is this," said Araminta. "We have two brains."

"You're joking," said Basil.

"I'm not. Every brontosaurus has two brains. One in its head and one in the middle of its back."

"Wow!" cried Basil. "Well, if I've got two brains and all the other kids have only got one, I must be twice as clever as them."

"You are, darling," said Araminta. "You are. So let's have no more of this cry-baby nonsense. Next time one of the children teases you, just think to yourself, 'I am twice as clever as you.'"

Not only did Basil think this, next
morning at playschool, but he also
thought that he was twice as big as
the other children.

"Did you have a nice time?" said
Araminta, when he came home.

"Smashing," said Basil.

"No tears?"

"Not mine," said Basil cheerily.

"You didn't tell anyone our secret?"

"Oh no," said Basil. "I didn't do much talking to the other kids. Actions speak louder than words."

Not long after this the playschool teacher, an elderly female stegosaurus, came to see Herb and Araminta.

"I'm sorry to bother you," she said, "but I'm a little worried about Basil."

"Not been blubbing again, has he?" said Herb.

"Oh no, *he* hasn't," said the stegosaurus. "In fact, recently he has grown greatly in confidence. At first he was rather nervous and the other children tended to make fun of him, but they don't any more. He's twice the boy he was."

"Can't think why," said Herb, but Araminta could.

"Indeed," the stegosaurus went on, "I fear that lately he's been throwing his weight about.

Boys will be boys, I know, but really Basil has become very rough. Only yesterday I had to send home a baby brachiosaurus with a badly bruised foot and a little trachodon with a black eye. I should be glad if you would speak to Basil about all this."

When the teacher had departed, Araminta said to Herb, "You must have a word with the boy."

"Why?" said Herb.

"You heard what the teacher said. He's been bullying the other children. He's obviously getting above himself."

At this point Basil appeared.

"What did old Steggy want?" he said.

"Tell him, Herb," said Araminta.

"Now look here, my boy," said Herb.

Basil looked.

"You listen to me."

Basil listened, but Herb, Araminta could see, had forgotten what he was talking about.

"Your father is very angry with you," she said. "You have been fighting. At playschool."

"That's right," said Herb. "Fighting. At playschool. Why?"

"Well, it's like this, Dad," said Basil. "The first day, the other kids teased me. They said I hadn't got a brain in my head, remember? And then Mum told me I had. And another in the middle of my back. Two brains! So I thought: I'm twice as clever as the rest as well as twice as big, so why not lean on them a bit? Not my fault if they get under my feet."

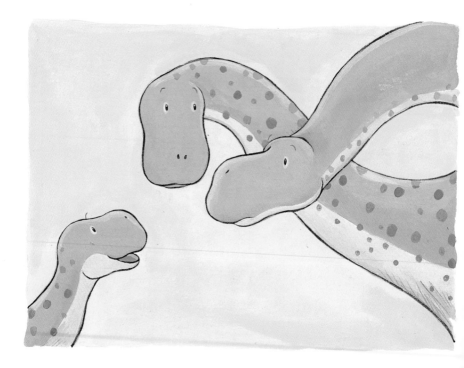

"You want to watch your step," said Herb.

"Daddy's right," said Araminta. "One of these days you'll get into real trouble. Now run along, I want to talk to your father."

"It's all my fault for telling him about having two brains," she said when Basil had gone. "He's too young. My parents didn't tell me till I was nearly grown up. How did you find out?"

"Oh, I don't know," said Herb. "I dare say I heard some of the chaps talking down in the swamp. When I was one of the gang. We used to talk a lot, down in the swamp."

"What about?" said Araminta.

"Waterweed, mostly," said Herb, and he pulled up a great mouthful and began to chomp.

Not long after this, Basil was expelled.

"I'm sorry," said the elderly stegosaurus, "but I can't have the boy in my class any longer. It isn't only his roughness, it's his rudeness. Do you know what he said to me today?"

"No," said Herb.

"What?" said Araminta.

"He said to me, 'I'm twice as clever as you are.'"

"Is he?" said Herb.

"Of course he isn't," said Araminta hastily. "He was just being silly and childish. I'm sure he won't be any trouble in the future."

"Not in my playschool he won't," said the stegosaurus and then, oddly, she used the very words that Araminta had used earlier.

"One of these days," she said, "he'll get into real trouble." And off she waddled, flapping her back plates angrily.

And one of those days, Basil did.

Being expelled from playschool hadn't worried him at all. What do I want with other dinosaurs? he thought. I'm far superior to them, with my two brains, one to work my neck and my front legs, one to work my back legs and my tail. Brontosauruses are twice as clever as other dinosaurs and I'm twice as clever as any other brontosaurus.

You couldn't say that Basil was big-headed, for that was almost the smallest part of him, but you could certainly say that he was boastful, conceited and arrogant.

"That boy!" said Araminta to Herb. "He's boastful, conceited and arrogant. He must get it from your side of the family, swaggering about and picking fights all the time. What does he think he is? A *Tyrannosaurus rex*?"

"What do you think you are?" Basil was saying at that very moment. He had come out of the lake where the family spent almost all their time, and set off for a walk.

He was ambling along, thinking what a fine fellow he was, when suddenly he saw a strange, smallish dinosaur standing in his path.

It was not like any dinosaur he had ever seen before. It stood upright on its hind legs, which were much bigger than its little forelegs, and it had a large head with large jaws and a great many teeth. But compared to Basil, who already weighed a couple of tonnes, it looked quite small, and he advanced upon it, saying in a rude tone, "What do you think you are?"

"I'm a *Tyrannosaurus rex*," said the
stranger.

"Never heard of you," said Basil.

"Lucky you."

"Why? What's so wonderful about
you? You can't even walk on four feet
like a decent dinosaur and you've only
got one brain. You'll be telling me
next that you don't eat waterweed like
we do."

"We don't," said the other. "We
only eat meat."

"What sort of meat?"

"Brontosaurus, mostly."

"Let's get this straight," said Basil. "Are you seriously telling me that you kill brontosauruses and eat them?"

"Yes."

"Don't make me laugh," said Basil. "I'm four times as big as you."

"Yes," said the youngster, "but my dad's four times as big as you. Oh, look, what a bit of luck. Here he comes!"

Basil looked up to see a terrifying sight.

Marching towards him on its huge hind legs was a towering, full-grown *Tyrannosaurus rex* with a mouthful of long razor-sharp teeth. All of a sudden Basil had two brainwaves.

Time I went, he thought. Sharpish. And as one brain sent a message rippling along to the other, he turned tail and made for the safety of the lake as fast as his legs could carry him. This was not very fast, as Basil's big body made him slow and clumsy on land. If the tyrannosaurus had been really hungry, he would have caught Basil without any trouble.

As it was, Basil reached the shore of the lake just in time and splashed frantically out to deeper water, where his parents, their long necks outstretched, were browsing on the weedy bottom.

Araminta was the first to look up.

"Hello, darling," she said. "Where have you been? Whatever's the matter? You're all of a doodah."

"Oh, Mummy, Mummy!" panted Basil. "It was awful! I went for a walk

and I was nearly eaten by a *Tyrannosaurus rex!*"

Herb raised his head in time to hear this.

"That'll teach you," he said.

"Teach me what, Dad?"

"Not to be so cocky," said Araminta. "Ever since I told you that secret you've been unbearable, Basil. I hope this will be a lesson to you."

"Oh, it will, Mummy, it will!" cried Basil. "I won't ever shoot my mouth off again."

"And don't go for walks," said his mother, "but keep close to the lake, where you'll be safe from the tyrannosaurus."

"In case he rex you," said Herb, and plunged his head under water again, while strings of bubbles rose as he laughed at his own joke.

"And if you want to grow up to be as big as your father," said Araminta, "there's one thing you must always remember to do."

"What's that, Mummy?" said Basil.

"Use your brains."

BLESSU
Dick King-Smith

The tall, flowering elephant-grasses give Blessu
hay fever. "BLESS YOU!" all the elephants cry
whenever little Blessu sneezes, which is very often.
Blessu grows slowly except for one part of him – his
trunk – and his sneeze becomes the biggest, loudest
sneeze in the world!

DUMPLING
Dick King-Smith

Dumpling wishes she could be long and
sausage-shaped like other dachshunds. When
a witch's cat grants her wish, Dumpling becomes
the longest dog ever.

ERIC'S ELEPHANT ON HOLIDAY
John Gatehouse

When Eric and his family go on holiday to
the seaside, Eric's elephant goes too. Everyone
is surprised – and rather cross – to find a big white
elephant on the beach. But the elephant soon amazes
them with her jumbo tricks and makes it a very
special holiday indeed!